THE HOLLOW LAND

By

WILLIAM MORRIS

British Library Cataloguing-in-Publication Data
A catalogue record for this book is available from
the British Library

Contents

WILLIAM MORRIS

William Morris was born in London, England in 1834. Arguably best known as a textile designer, he founded a design partnership which deeply influenced the decoration of churches and homes during the early 20th century. However, he is also considered an important Romantic writer and pioneer of the modern fantasy genre, being a direct influence on authors such as J. R. R. Tolkien. As well as fiction, Morris penned poetry and essays. Amongst his best-known works are *The Defence of Guenevere and Other Poems* (1858), *The Earthly Paradise* (1868–1870), *A Dream of John Ball* (1888), *News from Nowhere* (1890), and the fantasy romance *The Well at the World's End* (1896). Morris was also an important figure in British socialism, founding the Socialist League in 1884. He died in 1896, aged 62.

I

STRUGGLING IN THE WORLD

Do you know where it is – the Hollow Land?

I have been looking for it now so long, trying to find it again – the Hollow Land – for there I saw my love first.

I wish to tell you how I found it first of all; but I am old, my memory fails me: you must wait and let me think if I perchance can tell you how it happened.

Yea, in my ears is a confused noise of trumpet-blasts singing over desolate moors, in my ears and eyes a clashing and clanging of horse-hoofs, a ringing and glittering of steel; drawn-back lips, set teeth, shouts, shrieks and curses.

How was it that no one of us ever found it till that day? for it is near our country: but what time have we to look for it, or any good thing; with such biting carking cares hemming us in on every side – cares about great things – mighty things: mighty things, O my brothers! or rather little things enough, if we only knew it.

Lives past in turmoil, in making one another unhappy; in bitterest misunderstanding of our brothers' hearts, making those sad whom God has not made sad, – alas, alas! What chance for any of us to find the Hollow Land? What time even to look for it?

Yet who has not dreamed of it? Who, half miserable yet the while, for that he knows it is but a dream, has not felt the cool waves round his feet, the roses crowning him, and through the leaves of beech and lime the many whispering winds of the Hollow Land?

Now, my name was Florian, and my house was the house of the Lilies; and of that house was my father lord, and after him my eldest brother Arnald; and me they called Florian de Liliis.

Moreover, when my father was dead, there arose a feud between the Lilies' house and Red Harald; and this that follows is the history of it.

Lady Swanhilda, Red Harald's mother, was a widow, with one son, Red Harald; and when she had been in widowhood two years, being of princely blood, and besides comely and fierce, King Urrayne sent to demand her in marriage. And I remember seeing the procession leaving the town, when I was quite a child; and many young knights and squires attended the Lady Swanhilda as pages, and amongst them, Arnald, my eldest brother.

And as I gazed out of the window, I saw him walking by the side of her horse, dressed in white and gold very delicately; but as he went it chanced that he stumbled. Now he was one of those that held a golden canopy over the lady's head, so that it now sunk into wrinkles, and the lady had to bow her head full low, and even then the gold brocade caught in one of the long slim gold flowers that were wrought round about the crown she wore. She flushed up in her rage, and her smooth face went suddenly into the carven wrinkles of a wooden water-spout, and she caught at the brocade with her left hand, and pulled it away furiously, so that the warp and woof were twisted out of their place, and many gold threads were left dangling about the crown; but Swanhilda stared about when she rose, then smote my brother across the mouth with her gilded sceptre, and the red blood flowed all about his garments; yet he only turned exceeding pale, and dared say no word, though he was heir to the house of Lilies: but my small heart swelled with rage, and I vowed revenge, and, as it seems, he did too.

So when Swanhilda had been queen three years, she suborned many of King Urrayne's knights and lords, and slew her husband as he slept, and reigned in his stead. And her son, Harald, grew up to manhood, and was counted a strong knight, and well spoken of, by then I first put on my armour.

Then, one night, as I lay dreaming, I felt a hand laid on my face, and starting up saw Arnald before me fully armed. He said, 'Florian, rise and arm.' I did so, all but my helm, as he was.

He kissed me on the forehead; his lips felt hot and dry; and when they brought torches, and I could see his face plainly, I saw he was very pale. He said:

'Do you remember, Florian, this day sixteen years ago? It is a long time, but I shall never forget it unless this night blots out its memory.'

I knew what he meant, and because my heart was wicked, I rejoiced exceedingly at the thought of vengeance, so that I could not speak, but only laid my palm across his lips.

'Good; you have a good memory, Florian. See now, I waited long and long: I said at first, I forgive her; but when the news came concerning the death of the king, and how that she was shameless, I said I will take it as a sign, if God does not punish her within certain years, that he means me to do so; and I have been watching and watching now these two years for an opportunity, and behold it is come at last; and I think God has certainly given her into our hands, for she rests this night, this very Christmas eve, at a small walled town on the frontier, not two hours' gallop from this; they keep little ward there, and the night is wild: moreover, the prior of a certain house of monks, just without the walls, is my fast friend in this matter, for she has done him some great injury. In the courtyard below 150 knights and squires, all faithful and true, are waiting for us: one moment and we shall be gone.'

Then we both knelt down, and prayed God to give her into our hands: we put on our helms, and went down into the courtyard.

It was the first time I expected to use a sharp sword in anger, and I was full of joy as the muffled thunder of our horse-hoofs rolled through the bitter winter night.

In about an hour and a half we had crossed the frontier, and in half an hour more the greater part had halted in a wood near the Abbey, while I and a few others went up to the Abbey gates, and knocked loudly four times with my sword-hilt, stamping on the ground meantime. A long, low whistle answered me from within, which I in my turn answered: then the wicket opened, and a monk came out, holding a lantern. He seemed yet in the prime of his life, and was a tall, powerful man. He held the lantern to my face, then smiled, and said, 'The banners hang low.'

I gave the countersign, 'The crest is lopped off.'

'Good my son,' said he; 'the ladders are within here. I dare not trust any of the brethren to carry them for you, though they love not the witch either, but are timorsome.'

'No matter,' I said, 'I have men here.' So they entered and began to shoulder the tall ladders: the prior was very busy.

'You will find them just the right length, my son, trust me for that.' He seemed quite a jolly, pleasant man, I could not understand his nursing furious revenge; but his face darkened strangely whenever he happened to mention her name.

As we were starting he came and stood outside the gate, and putting his lantern down that the light of it might not confuse his sight, looked earnestly into the night, then said: 'The wind has fallen, the snow flakes get thinner and smaller every moment, in an hour it will be freezing hard, and will be quite clear; everything depends upon the surprise being complete; stop a few minutes yet, my son.' He went away chuckling, and returned presently with two more sturdy monks carrying something: they threw their burdens down before my feet, they consisted of all the white albs in the abbey: 'There, trust an old man, who has seen more than one stricken fight in his carnal days; let the men who scale the walls put these over their arms, and they will not be seen in the least. God make your sword sharp, my son.'

So we departed, and when I met Arnald again, he said that what the prior had done was well thought of; so we agreed that I should take thirty men, an old squire of our house, well skilled in war, along with them, scale the walls as quietly as possible, and open the gates to the rest.

I set off accordingly, after that with low laughing we had put the albs all over us, wrapping the ladders also in white. Then we crept very warily and slowly up the wall; the moat was frozen over, and on the ice the snow lay quite thick; we all thought that the guards must be careless enough, when they did not even take the trouble to break the ice in the moat. So we listened – there was no sound at all, the Christmas midnight mass had long ago been over, it was nearly three o'clock, and the moon began to clear. There was scarce any snow falling now, only a flake or two from some low hurrying cloud or other: the wind sighed gently about the round towers there, but it was bitter cold, for it had begun to freeze again. We listened for some minutes, about a quarter of an hour, I think, then at a sign from me, they raised the ladders carefully, muffled as they were at the top with swathings of wool. I mounted first, old Squire Hugh followed last; noiselessly we ascended, and soon stood altogether on the walls; then we carefully lowered the ladders again with long ropes; we got our swords and axes from out of the folds of our priests' raiments, and set forward, till we reached the first tower along the wall. The door was open, in the chamber at the top there was a fire slowly smouldering, nothing else; we passed through it, and began to go down the spiral staircase, I first, with my axe shortened in my hand. 'What if we were surprised there?' I thought, and I longed to be out in the air again. 'What if the door were fast at the bottom?'

As we passed the second chamber, we heard some one within snoring loudly: I looked in quietly, and saw a big man with long black hair, that fell off his pillow and swept the ground, lying snoring, with his nose turned up and his mouth open, but he seemed so sound asleep that we did not stop to slay him. Praise be! – the door was open. Without even a whispered word, without a pause, we went on along the streets, on the side that the drift had been on, because out garments were white, for the wind being very strong all that day, the houses on that side had caught in their cornices and carvings, and on the rough stone and wood of them, so much snow, that except here and there where the black walls grinned out, they were quite white. No man saw us as we stole along, / noiselessly because of the snow, till we stood within 100 yards of the gates and their house of guard. And we stood because we heard the voice of some one singing:

> 'Queen Mary's crown was gold,
>   King Joseph's crown was red,
> But Jesus' crown was diamond
>   That lit up all the bed.
>   *Mariae Virginis.*'

So they had some guards after all; this was clearly the sentinel that sang to keep the ghosts off. Now for a fight. We drew nearer, a few yards nearer, then stopped to free ourselves from our monks' clothes.

> 'Ships sail through the Heaven
>   With red banners dress'd,
> Carrying the planets seven
>   To see the white breast.
>   *Mariae Virginis.*'

7

Thereat he must have seen the waving of some alb or other as it shivered down to the ground, for his spear fell with a thud, and he seemed to be standing open-mouthed, thinking something about ghosts; then, plucking up heart of grace, he roared out like ten bull-calves, and dashed into the guard-house.

We followed smartly, but without hurry, and came up to the door of it just as some dozen half-armed men came tumbling out under our axes: thereupon, while our men slew them, I blew a great blast upon my horn, and Hugh with some others drew bolt and bar and swung the gates wide open.

Then the men in the guard-house understood they were taken in a trap, and began to stir with great confusion; so lest they should get quite waked and armed, I left Hugh at the gates with ten men, and myself led the rest into that house. There, while we slew all those that yielded not, came Arnald with the others, bringing our horses with them; then all the enemy threw their arms down. And we counted our prisoners and found them over fourscore; therefore, not knowing what to do with them (for they were too many to guard, and it seemed unknightly to slay them all), we sent up some bowmen to the walls, and turning our prisoners out of gates, bid them run for their lives, which they did fast enough, not knowing our numbers, and our men sent a few flights of arrows among them that they might not be undeceived.

Then the one or two prisoners that we had left told us, when we had crossed our axes over their heads, that the people of the good town would not willingly fight us, in that they hated the queen; that she was guarded at the palace by some fifty knights, and that beside, there were no others to oppose us in the town; so we set out for the palace, spears in hand.

We had not gone far, before we heard some knights coming, and soon, in a turn of the long street, we saw them riding towards us. When they caught sight of us they seemed astonished, drew rein, and stood in some confusion.

We did not slacken our pace for an instant, but rode right at them with a yell, to which I lent myself with all my heart.

After all they did not run away, but waited for us with their spears held out. I missed the man I had marked, or hit him rather just on the top of the helm; he bent back, and the spear slipped over his head, but my horse still kept on, and I felt presently such a crash that I reeled in my saddle, and felt mad. He had lashed out at me with his sword as I came on, hitting me in the ribs (for my arm was raised), but only flatlings.

I was quite wild with rage. I turned, almost fell upon him, caught him by the neck with both hands, and threw him under the horse-hoofs, sighing with fury. I heard Arnald's voice close to me, 'Well fought, Florian', and I saw his great stern face bare among the iron, for he had made a vow in remembrance of that blow always to fight unhelmed; I saw his great sword swinging, in wide gyres, and hissing as it started up, just as if it were alive and liked it.

So joy filled all my soul, and I fought with my heart, till the big axe I swung felt like nothing but a little hammer in my hand, except for its bitterness: and as for the enemy, they went down like grass, so that we destroyed them utterly, for those knights would neither yield nor fly, but died as they stood, so that some fifteen of our men also died there.

Then at last we came to the palace, where some grooms and such like kept the gates armed, but some ran, and some we took prisoners, one of whom died for sheer terror in our hands, being stricken by no wound, for he thought we would eat him.

These prisoners we questioned concerning the queen, and so entered the great hall.

There Arnald sat down in the throne on the dais, and laid his naked sword before him on the table: and on each side of him sat such knights as there was room for, and the others stood round about, while I took ten men, and went to look for Swanhilda.

I found her soon, sitting by herself in a gorgeous chamber. I almost pitied her when I saw her looking so utterly desolate and despairing; her beauty too had faded, deep lines cut through her face. But when I entered she knew who I was, and her look of intense hatred was so fiend-like, that it changed my pity into horror of her.

'Knight,' she said, 'who are you, and what do you want, thus discourteously entering my chamber?'

'I am Florian de Liliis, and I am to conduct you to judgment.'

She sprang up, 'Curse you and your whole house – you I hate worse than any – girl's face – guards! guards!' and she stamped on the ground, her veins on the forehead swelled, her eyes grew round and flamed out, as she kept crying for her guards, stamping the while, for she seemed quite mad.

Then at last she remembered that she was in the power of her enemies. She sat down, and lay with her face between her hands, and wept passionately.

'Witch,' I said between my closed teeth, 'will you come, or must we carry you down to the great hall?'

Neither would she come, but sat there, clutching at her dress and tearing her hair.

Then I said, 'Bind her, and carry her down.' And they did so.

I watched Arnald as we came in. There was no triumph on his stern white face, but resolution enough: he had made up his mind.

They placed her on a seat in the midst of the hall over against the dais. He said, 'Unbind her, Florian.' They did so. She raised her face, and glared defiance at us all, as though she would die queenly after all.

Then rose up Arnald and said, 'Queen Swanhilda, we judge you guilty of death, and because you are a queen and of a noble house, you shall be slain by my knightly sword, and I will even take the reproach of slaying a woman, for no other hand than mine shall deal the blow.'

Then she said, 'O false knight, show your warrant from God, man, or devil.'

'This warrant from God, Swanhilda,' he said, holding up his sword. 'Listen! Fifteen years ago, when I was just winning my spurs, you struck me, disgracing me before all the people; you cursed me, and meant that curse well enough. Men of the house of the Lilies, what sentence for that?'

'Death!' they said.

'Listen! Afterwards you slew my cousin, your husband, treacherously, in the most cursed way, stabbing him in the throat, as the stars in the canopy above him looked down on the shut eyes of him. Men of the house of the Lilies, what sentence for that?'

'Death!' they said.

'Do you hear them, Queen? There is warrant from man. For the devil, I do not reverence him enough to take warrant from him, but, as I look at that face of yours, I think that even he has left you.'

And indeed just then all her pride seemed to leave her: she fell from the chair, and wallowed on the ground moaning; she wept like a child, so that the tears lay on the oak floor; she prayed for another month of life; she came to me and kneeled, and kissed my feet, and prayed piteously, so that water ran out of her mouth.

But I shuddered, and drew away; it was like having an adder about one; I could have pitied her had she died bravely, but for one like her to whine and whine! – pah!

Then from the dais rang Arnald's voice, terrible, much changed. 'Let there be an end of all this.' And he took his sword and strode through the hall towards her; she rose from the ground and stood up, stooping a little, her head sunk between her shoulders, her black eyes turned up and gleaming, like a tigress about to spring. When he came within some six paces of her something in his eye daunted her, or perhaps the flashing of his terrible sword in the torch-light- she threw her arms up with a great shriek, and dashed screaming about the hall. Arnald's lip never once curled with any scorn, no line in his face changed: he said, 'Bring her here and bind her.'

But when one came up to her to lay hold on her she first of all ran at him, hitting with her head in the belly. Then while he stood doubled up for want of breath, and staring with his head up, she caught his sword from the girdle, and cut him across the shoulders, and many others she wounded sorely before they took her.

Then Arnald stood by the chair to which she was bound, and poised his sword, and there was a great silence.

Then he said, 'Men of the house of the Lilies, do you justify me in this? Shall she die?' Straightaway rang a great shout through the hall, but before it died away the sword had swept round, and therewithal was there no such thing as Swanhilda left upon the earth, for in no battle-field had Arnald struck a truer blow. Then he turned to the few servants of the palace and said, 'Go now, bury his accursed woman, for she is a king's daughter.' Then to us all, 'Now knights, to horse and away, that we may reach the good town by about dawn.' So we mounted and rode off.

What a strange Christmas-day that was, for there, about nine o'clock in the morning, rode Red Harald into the good town to demand vengeance. He went at once to the king, and the king promised that before nightfall that very day the matter should be judged; albeit the king feared somewhat, because every third man you met in the streets had a blue cross on his shoulder, and some likeness of a lily, cut out or painted, stuck in his hat; and this blue cross and lily were the bearings of our house, called 'De Liliis'. Now we had seen Red Harald pass through the streets, with a white banner borne before him, to show that he came peaceably as for this time; but I know he was thinking of other things than peace.

And he was called Red Harald first at this time, because over all his arms he wore a great scarlet cloth, that fell in heavy folds about his horse and all about him. Then, as he passed our house, someone pointed it out to him, rising there with its carving and its barred marble, but stronger than many a castle on the hill-tops, and its great overhanging battlement cast a mighty shadow down the wall and across the street; and above all rose the great tower, a banner floating proudly from the top, whereon was emblazoned on a white ground a blue cross, and on a blue ground four white lilies. And now faces were gazing from all the windows, and all the battlements were thronged; so Harald turned, and rising in his stirrups, shook his clenched fist at our house; as he did so, the east wind, coming down the street, caught up the corner of that scarlet cloth and drove it over his face, and therewithal disordering his long black hair, well nigh choked him, so that he bit both his hair and that cloth.

So from base to cope rose a mighty shout of triumph and defiance, and he passed on.

Then Arnald caused it to be cried that all those who loved the good house of the Lilies should go to mass that morning in Saint Mary's Church, hard by our house. Now this church belonged to us, and the abbey that served it, and always we appointed the abbot of it on condition that our trumpets should sound all together when on high masses they sing the 'Gloria in Excelsis'. It was the largest and most beautiful of all the churches in town, and had two exceeding high towers, which you could see from far off, even when you saw not the town or any of its other towers: and in one of these towers were twelve great bells, named after the twelve Apostles, one name being written on each one of them; as Peter, Matthew, and so on; and in the other tower was one great bell only, much larger than any of the others, and which was called Mary. Now this bell was never rung but when our house was in great danger, and it had this legend on it: 'When Mary rings the earth shakes'; and indeed from this we took our war cry, which was, 'Mary rings'; somewhat justifiable indeed, for the last time that Mary rang, on that day before nightfall there were 4000 bodies to be buried, which bodies wore neither cross nor lily.

So Arnald gave me in charge to tell the abbot to cause Mary to be tolled for an hour before mass that day.

The abbot leaned on my shoulder as I stood within the tower and looked at the twelve monks laying their hands to the ropes. Far up in the dimness I saw the wheel before it began to swing round about; then it moved a little. The twelve men bent down to the earth and a roar rose that shook the tower from base to spire-vane: backwards and forwards swept the wheel, as Mary now looked downwards towards earth, now looked up at the shadowy cone of the spire, shot across by bars of light from the dormers.

And the thunder of Mary was caught up by the wind and carried through all the country; and when the good man heard it, he said goodbye to wife and child, slung his shield behind his back, and set forward with his spear sloped over his shoulder. Many a time, as he walked toward the good town, he tightened the belt that went about his waist, that he might stride the faster, so long and furiously did Mary toll.

And before the great bell, Mary, had ceased ringing, all the ways were full of armed men.

But at each door of the church of Saint Mary stood a row of men armed with axes, and when any came, meaning to go into the church, the two first of these would hold their axes (whose helves were about four feet long) over his head, and would ask him, 'Who went over the moon last night?' then if he answered nothing or at random they would bid him turn back, which he for the more part would be ready enough to do; but some, striving to get through that row of men, were slain outright;

but if he were one of those that were friends to the house of the Lilies he would answer to that question, 'Mary and John.'

By the time the mass began the whole church was full, and in the nave and transept thereof were 3000 men, all of our house and all armed. But Arnald and myself, and Squire Hugh, and some others sat under a gold-fringed canopy near the choir; and the abbot said mass, having his mitre on his head. Yet, as I watched him, it seemed to me that he must have something on beneath his priest's vestments, for he looked much fatter than usual, being really a tall lithe man.

Now, as they sang the 'Kyrie', some one shouted from the other end of the church, 'My lord Arnald, they are slaying our people without;' for, indeed, all the square about the church was full of our people, who for the press had not been able to enter, and were standing there in no small dread of what might come to pass.

Then the abbot turned round from the altar, and began to fidget with the fastenings of his rich robes.

And they made a lane for us up to the west door; then I put on my helm and we began to go up the nave, when suddenly the singing of the monks and all stopped. I heard a clinking and a buzz of voices in the choir. I turned, and saw that the bright noon sun was shining on the gold of the priest's vestments, as they lay on the floor and on the mail that the priests carried.

So we stopped, the choir gates swung open, and the abbot marched out at the head of *his* men, all fully armed, and began to strike up the psalm 'Exsurgat Deus'.

When we got to the west door, there was indeed a tumult, but as yet no slaying; the square was all a-flicker with steel, and we beheld a great body of knights, at the head of them Red Harald and the king, standing over against us; but our people, pressed against the houses, and into the corners of the square, were, some striving to enter the doors, some beside themselves with rage, shouting out to the others to charge; withal, some were pale and some were red with the blood that had gathered to the wrathful faces of them.

Then said Arnald to those about him, 'Lift me up.' So they laid a great shield on two lances, and these four men carried, and thereon stood Arnald, and gazed about him.

Now the king was unhelmed, and his white hair (for he was

an old man) flowed down behind him on to his saddle; but Arnald's hair was cut short, and was red.

And all the bells rang.

Then the king said, 'O Arnald of the Lilies, will you settle this quarrel by the judgment of God?'

And Arnald thrust up his chin, and said, 'Yea.'

'How then,' said the king, 'and where?'

'Will it please you try now?' said Arnald.

Then the king understood what he meant, and took in his hand from behind tresses of his long white hair, twisting them round his hand in his wrath, but yet said no word, till I suppose his hair put him in mind of something, and he raised it in both his hands above his head, and shouted out aloud. 'O knights, hearken to this traitor.' Whereat, indeed, the lances began to move ominously. But Arnald spoke.

'O you king and lords, what have we to do with you? Were we not free in the old time, up among the hills there? Wherefore give way, and we will go to the hills again; and if any man try to stop us, his blood be on his own head; wherefore now,' (and he turned) 'all you of the house of the Lilies, both soldiers and monks, let us go forth together fearing nothing, for I think there is not bone enough or muscle enough in these fellows here that have a king that they should stop us withal, but only skin and fat.'

And truly, no man dared to stop us, and we went.

II

FALLING IN THE WORLD

Now at that time we drove cattle in Red Harald's land.

And we took no hoof but from the lords and rich men, but of these we had a mighty drove, both oxen and sheep, and horses, and besides, even hawks and hounds, and huntsman or two to take care of them.

And, about noon, we drew away from the corn-lands that lay beyond the pastures, and mingled with them, and reached a wide moor, which was called 'Goliah's Land'. I scarce know why, except that it belonged neither to Red Harald nor us, but was debatable.

And the cattle began to go slowly, and our horses were tired, and the sun struck down very hot upon us, for there was no shadow, and the day was cloudless.

All about the edge of the moor, except on the side from which we had come, was a rim of hills, not very high, but very rocky and steep. Otherwise the moor itself was flat. And through these hills was one pass, guarded by our men, which pass led to the hill castle of the Lilies.

It was not wonderful that, of this moor, many wild stories were told, being such a strange lonely place; some of them one knew, alas! to be over true. In the old time, before we went to the good town, this moor had been the mustering place of our people, and our house had done deeds enough of blood and horror to turn our white lilies red, and our blue cross to a fiery one. But some of those wild tales I never believed; they had to do mostly with men losing their way without any apparent cause (for there were plenty of landmarks), finding some well-known spot, and then, just beyond it, a place they had never even dreamed of.

'Florian! Florian!' said Arnald. 'For God's sake, stop! As every one else is stopping to look at the hills yonder. I always thought there was a curse upon us. What does God mean by shutting us up here? Look at the cattle; O Christ, they have found it out too! See, some of them are turning to run back again towards Harald's land. Oh! unhappy, unhappy, from that day forward!'

He leaned forward, rested his head on his horse's neck, and wept like a child.

I felt so irritated with him, that I could almost have slain him then and there. Was he mad? Had these wild doings of ours turned his strong wise head?

'Are you my brother Arnald, that I used to think such a grand man when I was a boy?' I said. 'Or are you changed too, like everybody, and everything else? What do *you* mean?'

'Look! Look!' he said, grinding his teeth in agony.

I raised my eyes: where was the one pass between the rim of stern rocks? Nothing: the enemy behind us – that grim wall in front: what wonder that each man looked in his fellow's face for help, and found it not. Yet I refused to believe that there was any truth either in the wild stories that I had heard when I was a boy, or in this story told me so clearly by my eyes now.

I called out cheerily, 'Hugh, come here!' He came. 'What do you think of this? Some mere dodge on Harald's part? Are we cut off?'

'Think, Sir Florian? God forgive me for ever thinking at all; I have given up that long and long ago, because thirty years ago I thought this, that the house of Lilies would deserve anything in the way of bad fortune that God would send them: so I gave up thinking, and took to fighting. But if you think that Harald had anything to do with this, why – why – in God's name, I wish *I* could think so!'

I felt a dull weight on my heart. Had our house been the devil's servants all along? I thought we were God's servants.

The day was very still, but what little wind there was, was at our backs. I watched Hugh's face, not being able to answer him. He was the cleverest man at war that I have known, either before or since that day: sharper than any hound in ear and scent, clearer sighted than any eagle. He was listening now intently. I saw a slight smile cross his face; heard him mutter, 'Yes! I think so: verily that is better, a great deal better.' Then he stood up in his stirrups, and shouted, 'Hurrah for the Lilies! Mary rings!'

'Mary rings!' I shouted, though I did not know the reason for his exultation. My brother lifted his head, and smiled too, grimly. Then as I listened I heard clearly the sound of a trumpet, and enemy's trumpet too.

'After all, it was only mist, or some such thing,' I said, for the pass between the hills was clear enough now.

'Hurrah! Only mist,' said Arnald, quite elated. 'Mary rings!' and we all began to think of fighting, for after all what joy is equal to that?

There were 500 of us: 200 spears, the rest archers, and both archers and men at arms were picked men.

'How many of them are we to expect?' said I.

'Not under a thousand, certainly, probably more, Sir Florian.' (My brother Arnald, by the way, had knighted me before we left the good town, and Hugh liked to give me the handle to my name. How was it, by the way, that no one had ever made *him* a knight?)

'Let every one look to his arms and horse, and come away from these silly cows' sons!' shouted Arnald.

Hugh said, 'They will be here in an hour, fair Sir.'

So we got clear of the cattle, and dismounted, and both ourselves took food and drink, and our horses; afterwards we tightened our saddle-girths, shook our great pots of helmets on, except Arnald, whose rusty-red hair had been his only head-piece in battle for years and years, and stood with our spears close by our horses, leaving room for the archers to retreat between our ranks; and they got their arrows ready, and planted their stakes before a little peat moss. And there we waited, and saw their pennons at last floating high above the corn of the fertile land, then heard their many horse-hoofs ring upon the hard-parched moor, and the archers began to shoot.

It had been a strange battle. We had never fought better, and yet withal it had ended in a retreat; indeed all along every man but Arnald and myself, even Hugh, had been trying at least to get the enemy between him and the way toward the pass; and now we were all drifting that way, the enemy trying to cut us off, but never able to stop us, because he could only throw small bodies of men in our way, whom we scattered and put to flight in their turn.

I never cared less for my life than then; indeed, in spite of all my boasting and hardness of belief, I should have been happy to have died, such a strange weight of apprehension was on me; and yet I got no scratch even. I had soon put off my great helm, and was fighting in my mail-coif only: and here I swear that three knights together charged me, aiming at my bare face, yet never touched me. For, as for one, I put his lance aside with my sword, and the other two in some most wonderful manner got their spears locked in each other's armour, and so had to submit to be knocked off their horses.

And we still neared the pass, and began to see distinctly the ferns that grew on the rocks, and the fair country between the rift in them, spreading our there, blue-shadowed.

Whereupon came a great rush of men of both sides, striking side blows at each other, spitting, cursing, and shrieking, as they tore away like a herd of wild hogs. So, being careless of life, as I said, I drew rein, and turning my horse, waited quietly for them, and I knotted the reins, and laid them on the horse's neck, and stroked him, that he whinnied, then got both my hands to my sword.

Then, as they came on, I noted hurriedly that the first man was one of Arnald's men, and one of our men behind him leaned forward to prod him with his spear, but could not reach so far, till he himself was run through the eye with a spear, and throwing his arms up fell dead with a shriek. Also I noted concerning this first man that the laces of his helmet were loose, and when he saw me he lifted his *left* hand to his head, took off his helm and cast it at me, and still tore on; the helmet flew over my head, and I sitting still there, swung out, hitting him on the neck; his head flew right off, for the mail no more held than a piece of silk.

'Mary rings,' and my horse whinnied again, and we both of us went at it, and fairly stopped that rout, so that there was a knot of quite close and desperate fighting, wherein we had the best of that fight and slew most of them, albeit my horse was slain and my mail-coif cut through. Then I bade a squire fetch me another horse, and began meanwhile to upbraid those knights for running in such a strange disorderly race, instead of standing and fighting cleverly.

Moreover we had drifted even in this successful fight still nearer to the pass, so that the conies who dwelt there were beginning to consider whether they should not run into their holes.

But one of those knights said: 'Be not angry with me, Sir Florian, but do you think you will go to Heaven?'

'The saints! I hope so,' I said, but one who stood near him whispered to him to hold his peace, so I cried out:

'O friend! I hold this world and all therein so cheap now, that I see not anything in it but shame which can any longer anger me; wherefore speak out.'

'Then, Sir Florian, men say that at your christening some fiend took on him the likeness of a priest and strove to baptise you in the Devil's name, but God had mercy on you so that the fiend could not choose but baptise you in the name of the most holy Trinity: and yet men say that you hardly believe any doctrine such as other men do, and will at the end only go to Heaven round about as it were, not at all by the intercession of

Our Lady; they say to that you can see no ghosts or other wonders, whatever happens to other Christian men.'

I smiled. 'Well, friend, I scarcely call this a disadvantage, moreover what has it to do with the matter in hand?'

How was this in Heaven's name? We had been quite still, resting while this talk was going on, but we could hear the hawks chattering from the rocks, we were so close now.

And my heart sank within me, there was no reason why this should not be true; there was no reason why anything should not be true.

'This, Sir Florian,' said the knight again, 'how would you feel inclined to fight if you thought that everything about you was mere glamour: this earth here, the rocks, the sun, the sky? I do not know where I am for certain: I do not know if I have been fighting men or only *simulacra* – but I think, we all think, that we have been led into some Devil's trap or other, and – and – may God forgive me my sins! – I wish I had never been born.'

There now! he was weeping – they all wept – how strange it was to see those rough, bearded men blubbering there, and snivelling till the tears ran over their armour and mingled with the blood, so that it dropped down to the earth in a dim, dull, red rain.

My eyes indeed were dry, but then so was my heart. I felt far worse than weeping came to, but nevertheless I spoke cheerily.

'Dear friends, where are your old men's hearts gone to now? See now! This is a punishment for our sins, is it? Well, for our forefathers' sins or our own? If the first, O brothers, be very sure that if we bear it manfully God will have something very good in store for us hereafter; but if for our sins, is it not certain that He cares for us yet, for note that He suffers the wicked to go their own ways pretty much. Moreover, brave men, brothers, ought to be the masters of *simulacra* – come, is it so hard to die once for all?'

Still no answer came from them; they sighed heavily only. I heard the sound of more than one or two swords as they rattled back to the scabbards: nay, one knight, stripping himself of surcoat and hauberk, and drawing his dagger, looked at me with a grim smile, and said, 'Sir Florian, do so!' Then he drew the dagger across his throat and he fell back dead.

They shuddered, those brave men, and crossed themselves. And I had no heart to say a word more, but mounted the horse which had been brought to me and rode away slowly for a few yards. Then I became aware that there was a great silence over the whole field.

So I lifted my eyes and looked, and behold no man struck at another.

Then from out of a band of horsemen came Harald, and he was covered all over with a great scarlet cloth as before, put on over the head, and flowing all about his horse, but rent with the fight. He put off his helm and drew back his mail-coif, then took a trumpet from the hand of a herald and blew strongly.

And in the midst of his blast I heard a voice call out: 'O Florian! Come and speak to me for the last time!'

So when I turned I beheld Arnald standing by himself, but near him stood Hugh and ten others with drawn swords.

Then I wept, and so went to him weeping; and he said, 'Thou seest, brother, that we must die, and I think by some horrible and unheard-of death, and the house of the Lilies is just dying too; and now I repent me of Swanhilda's death; now I know that it was a poor cowardly piece of revenge, instead of a brave act of justice. Thus has God shown us the right.

'O Florian! curse me! So will it be straighter; truly thy mother when she bore thee did not think of this; rather saw thee in the tourney at this time, in her fond hopes, glittering with gold and doing knightly deeds; or else mingling thy brown locks with the golden hair of some maiden weeping for the love of thee. God forgive me! God forgive me!'

'What harm, brother?' I said. 'This is only failing in the world. What if we had not failed? In a little while it would have made no difference. Truly just now I felt very miserable, but now it has passed away, and I am happy.'

'O brave heart!' he said. 'Yet we shall part just now, Florian, farewell.'

'The road is long,' I said. 'Farewell.'

Then we kissed each other, and Hugh and the others wept.

Now all this time the trumpets had been ringing, ringing, great doleful peals, then they ceased, and above all sounded Red Harald's voice.

(So I looked round towards that pass, and when I looked I

no longer doubted any of those wild tales of glamour concerning Goliah's Land, for though the rocks were the same, and though the conies still stood gazing at the doors of their dwellings, though the hawks still cried out shrilly, though the ferns still shook in the wind, yet beyond, oh such a land! not to be described by any because of its great beauty, lying, a great *hollow* land, the rocks going down on this side in precipices, then reaches and reaches of loveliest country, trees and flowers, and corn, then the hills, green and blue, and purple, till their ledges reached the white snowy mountains at last. Then with all manner of strange feelings, 'my heart in the midst of my body was even like melting wax.')

'O you house of the Lilies! you are conquered – yet I will take vengeance only on a few, therefore let all those who wish to live come and pile their swords, and shields, and helms behind me in three great heaps, and swear fealty afterwards to me; yes, all but the false knights Arnald and Florian.'

We were holding each other's hands and gazing, and we saw all our knights, yea, all but Squire Hugh and his ten heroes, pass over the field singly, or in groups of three or four, with their heads hanging down in shame, and they cast down their notched swords and dinted, lilied shields, and brave-crested helms into three great heaps behind Red Harald, then stood behind, no man speaking to his fellow, or touching him.

Then dolefully the great trumpets sang over the dying house of the Lilies, and Red Harald led his men forward, but slowly: on they came, spear and mail glittering in the sunlight; and I turned and looked at that good land, and a shuddering delight seized my soul.

But I felt my brother's hand leave mine, and saw him turn his horse's head and ride swiftly towards the pass that was a strange pass now.

And at the edge he stopped, turned round and called out aloud, 'I pray thee, Harald, forgive me! Now farewell all!'

Then the horse gave one bound forward, and we heard the poor creature's scream when he felt that he must die, and we heard afterwards (for we were near enough for that even) a clang and a crash.

So I turned me about to Hugh, and he understood me though I could not speak.

We shouted all together, 'Mary rings!' then laid our bridles on the necks of our horses, spurred forward, and – in five minutes they were all slain, and I was down among the horse-hoofs.

Not slain though, not wounded. Red Harald smiled grimly when he saw me rise and lash out again; he and some ten others dismounted, and holding their long spears out, I went back – back, back – I saw what it meant, and sheathed my sword, and their laughter rolled all about me, and I too smiled.

Presently they all stopped, and I felt the last foot of turf giving under my feet; I looked down and saw the crack there widening. Then in a moment I fell, and a cloud of dust and earth rolled after me; then again their mirth rose into thunder-peals of laughter. But through it all I heard Red Harald shout, 'Silence! Evil dogs!'

For as I fell I stretched out my arms, and caught a tuft of yellow broom some three feet from the brow, and hung there by the hands, my feet being loose in the air.

Then Red Harald came and stood on the precipice above me, his great axe over his shoulder; and he looked down on me not ferociously, almost kindly, while the wind from the Hollow Land blew about his red raiment, tattered and dusty now.

And I felt happy, though it pained me to hold straining by the broom, yet I said, 'I will hold out to the last.'

It was not long. The plant itself gave way and I fell, and as I fell, I fainted.

III

LEAVING THE WORLD
First Canto

I had thought when I fell that I should never wake again; but I woke at last: for a long time I was quite dizzied and could see nothing at all. Horrible doubts came creeping over me; I half expected to see presently great half-formed shapes come rolling up to me to crush me, some thing fiery, not strange, too utterly horrible to be strange, but utterly vile and ugly, the sight of which would have killed me when I was upon the earth, come rolling up to torment me. In fact I doubted if I were in hell.

I knew I deserved to be, but I prayed, and then it came into my mind that I could not pray if I were in hell.

Also there seemed to be a cool green light all about me, which was sweet.

Then presently I heard a glorious voice ring out clear, close to me:

> 'Christ keep the Hollow Land
> Through the sweet spring-tide,
> When the apple-blossoms bless
> The lowly bent hillside.'

Thereat my eyes were slowly unsealed, and I saw the blessedest sight I have ever seen before or since: for I saw my Love.

She sat about five yards from me on a great grey stone that had much moss on it, one of the many scattered along the side of the stream by which I lay. She was clad in loose white raiment close to her hands and throat; her feet were bare, her hair hung loose a long way down, but some of it lay on her knees. I said 'white' raiment, but long spikes of light scarlet went down from the throat, lost here and there in the shadows of the folds, and growing smaller and smaller, died before they reached her feet.

I was lying with my head resting on soft moss that some one had gathered and placed under me. She, when she saw me moving and awake, came and stood over me with a gracious smile. She was so lovely and tender to look at, and so kind, yet withal no one, man or woman, had ever frightened me half so much.

She was not fair in white and red, like many beautiful women are, being rather pale, but like ivory for smoothness, and her hair was quite golden, not light yellow, but dusky golden.

I tried to get up on my feet, but was too weak, and sank back again. She said:

'No, not just yet. Do not trouble yourself or try to remember anything just at present.'

There withal she kneeled down, and hung over me closer.

'Tomorrow you may, perhaps, have something hard to do or bear, I know, but now you must be as happy as you can be, quietly happy. Why did you start and turn pale when I came to you? Do you not know who I am? Nay, but you do, I see; and I have been waiting here so long for you; so you must have expected to see me. You cannot be frightened of me, are you?'

But I could not answer a word. But all the time strange knowledge, strange feelings were filling my brain and my heart, she said:

'You are tired. Rest, and dream happily.'

So she sat by me, and sang to lull me to sleep, while I turned on my elbow, and watched the waving of her throat: and the singing of all the poets I had ever heard, and of many others too, not born till years long after I was dead, floated all about me as she sang, and I did indeed dream happily.

When I awoke it was the time of the cold dawn, and the colours were gathering themselves together, whereat in fatherly approving fashion the sun sent all across the east long bars of scarlet and orange that after faded through yellow to green and blue.

And she sat by me still; I think she had been sitting there and singing all the time; all through hot yesterday, for I had been sleeping day-long and night-long, all through the falling evening under moonlight and starlight the night through.

And now it was dawn, and I think too that neither of us had moved at all; for the last thing I remembered before I went to sleep was the tips of her fingers brushing my cheek, as she knelt over me with down-drooping arm, and still now I felt them there. Moreover she was just finishing some fainting measure that died before it had time to get painful in its passion.

Dear Lord! how I loved her! Yet did I not dare to touch her, or even speak to her. She smiled with delight when she saw I was awake again, and slid down her hand on to mine, but some shuddering dread made me draw it away again hurriedly; then I saw the smile leave her face. What would I not have given for courage to hold her body quite tight to mine? But I was so weak. She said:

'Have you been very happy?'

'Yea,' I said.

It was the first word I had spoken there, and my voice sounded strange.

'Ah!' she said. 'You will talk more when you get used to the air of the Hollow Land. Have you been thinking of your past life at all? If not, try to think of it. What thing in Heaven or Earth do you wish for most?'

Still I said no word; but she said in a wearied way:

'Well now, I think you will be strong enough to get to your feet and walk. Take my hand and try.'

Therewith she held it out. I strove hard to be brave enough to take it, but could not; I only turned away shuddering, sick, and grieved to the heart's core of me. Then struggling hard with hand and knee and elbow, I scarce rose, and stood up totteringly, while she watched me sadly, still holding out her hand.

But as I rose, in my swinging to and fro the steel sheath of my sword struck her on the hand so that the blood flowed from it, which she stood looking at for a while, then dropped it downwards, and turned to look at me, for I was going.

Then as I walked she followed me, so I stopped and turned and said almost fiercely:

'I am going alone to look for my brother.'

The vehemence with which I spoke, or something else, burst some blood vessel within my throat, and we both stood there with the blood running from us on to the grass and summer flowers.

She said: 'If you find him, wait with him till I come.'

'Yea,' and I turned and left her, following the course of the stream upwards, and as I went I heard her low singing that almost broke my heart for its sadness.

And I went painfully because of my weakness, and because also of the great stones; and sometimes I went along a spot of earth where the river had been used to flow in flood-time, and which was now bare of everything but stones; and the sun, now risen high, poured down on everything a great flood of fierce light and scorching heat, and burnt me sorely, so that I almost fainted.

But about noontide I entered a wood close by the stream, a beech-wood, intending to rest myself. The herbage was thin and scattered there, sprouting up from amid the leaf-sheaths and nuts of the beeches, which had fallen year after year on that same spot. The outside boughs swept low down; the air itself seemed green when you entered within the shadow of the branches; they over-roofed the place so with tender green, only here and there showing spots of blue.

But what lay at the foot of a great beech tree but some dead knight in armour, only the helmet off? A wolf was prowling round about it, who ran away snarling when he saw me coming.

So I went up to that dead knight, and fell on my knees before him, laying my head on his breast, for it was Arnald.

He was quite cold, but had not been dead for very long. I would not believe him dead, but went down to the stream and brought him water, tried to make him drink – what would you do? He was as dead as Swanhilda. Neither came there any answer to my cries that afternoon but the moaning of the wood-doves in the beeches.

So then I sat down and took his head on my knees, and closed the eyes, and wept quietly while the sun sank lower.

But a little after sunset I heard a rustle through the leaves, that was not the wind, and looking up my eyes met the pitying eyes of that maiden.

Something stirred rebelliously within me. I ceased weeping, and said: 'It is unjust, unfair. What right had Swanhilda to live? Did not God give her up to us? How much better was he than ten Swanhildas? And look you – see! – he is DEAD!'

Now this I shrieked out, being mad; and though I trembled when I saw some stormy wrath that vexed her very heart and loving lips gathering on her face, I yet sat there looking at her and screaming, screaming, till all the place rang.

But when growing hoarse and breathless I ceased, she said, with straightened brow and scornful mouth:

'So! Bravely done! Must I then, though I am a woman, call you a liar, for saying God is unjust? You to punish her, had not God then punished her already? How many times when she woke in the dead night do you suppose she missed seing King Urrayne's pale face and hacked head lying on the pillow by her side? Whether by night or day, what things but screams did she hear when the wind blew loud round about the palace corners? And did not that face too, often come before her, pale and bleeding as it was long ago, and gaze at her from unhappy eyes! Poor eyes! With changed purpose in them – no more hope of converting the world when that blow was once struck; truly it was very wicked – no more dreams, but only fierce struggles with the Devil for very life, no more dreams but failure at last, and death, happier so in the Hollow Land.'

She grew so pitying as she gazed at his dead face that I began to weep again unreasonably, while she saw not that I was weeping, but looked only on Arnald's face, but after turned on me frowning.

'Unjust! Yes, truly unjust enough to take away life and all hope from her. You have done a base cowardly act, you and your brother here, disguise it as you may. You deserve all God's judgment – you—'

But I turned my eyes and wet face to her and said:

'Do not curse me – there – do not look like Swanhilda, for see now, you said at first that you have been waiting long for me. Give me your hand now, for I love you so.'

Then she came and knelt by where I sat, and I caught her in my arms and she prayed to be forgiven.

'O, Florian! I have indeed waited long for you, and when I saw you my heart was filled with joy, but you would neither touch me nor speak to me, so that I became almost mad. Forgive me, we will be so happy now. O! do you know this is what I have been waiting for all these years? It made me glad, I know, when I was a little baby in my mother's arms, to think I was born for this; and afterwards, as I grew up, I used to watch every breath of wind through the beech-boughs, every turn of the silver poplar leaves, thinking it might be you or some news of you.'

Then I rose and drew her up with me; but she knelt again by my brother's side, and kissed him, and said:

'O brother! The Hollow Land is only second best of the places God has made, for Heaven also is the work of His hand.'

Afterwards we dug a deep grave among the beech-roots and there we buried Arnald de Liliis.

And I have never seen him since, scarcely even in dreams. Surely God has had mercy on him, for he was very leal and true and brave; he loved many men, and was kind and gentle to his friends, neither did he hate any but Swanhilda.

But as for us two, Margaret and me, I cannot tell you concerning our happiness, such things cannot be told. Only this I know: that we abode continually in the Hollow Land until I lost it.

Moreover this I can tell you. Margaret was walking with me, as she often walked near the place where I had first seen her. Presently we came upon a woman sitting, dressed in scarlet and gold raiment, with her head laid down on her knees; likewise we heard her sobbing.

'Margaret, who is she?' I said. 'I knew not that any dwelt in the Hollow Land but us two only.'

She said, 'I know not who she is, only sometimes, these many years, I have seen her scarlet robe flaming from far away, amid the quiet green grass: but I was never so near her as this. Florian, I am afraid: let us come away.'

Second Canto

Such a horrible grey November day it was, the fog-smell all about creeping into our very bones.

And I sat there, trying to recollect, at any rate something, under those fir-trees that I ought to have known so well.

Just think now: I had lost my best years somewhere, for I was past the prime of life, my hair and beard were scattered with white, my body was growing weaker, my memory of all things was very faint.

My raiment, purple and scarlet and blue once, was so stained that you could scarce call it any colour, was so tattered that it scarce covered my body, though it seemed once to have fallen in heavy folds to my feet, and still, when I rose to walk, though the miserable November mist lay in great drops upon my bare breast, yet was I obliged to wind my raiment over my arm, it draggled so (wretched, slimy, textureless thing!) in the brown mud.

On my head was a light morion, which pressed on my brow and pained me, so I put my hand up to take it off. But when I touched it I stood still in my walk shuddering. I nearly fell to the earth with shame and sick horror, for I laid my hand on a lump of slimy earth with worms coiled up in it. I could scarce forbear from shrieking, but breathing such a prayer as I could think of, I raised my hand again and seized it firmly. Worse horror still! The rust had eaten it into holes, and I gripped my own hair as well as the rotting steel, the sharp edge of which cut into my fingers; but setting my teeth, gave a great wrench, for I knew that if I let go of it then, no power on the earth or under it could make me touch it again. God be praised! I tore it off and cast it far from me; I saw the earth, and the worms and green weeds and sun-begotten slime, whirling out from it radiatingly, as it spun round about.

I was girt with a sword too, the leathern belt of which had shrunk and squeezed my waist: dead leaves had gathered in knots about the buckles of it, the gilded handle was encrusted with clay in many parts, the velvet sheath miserably worn.

But, verily, when I took hold of the hilt, and dreaded lest instead of a sword I should find a serpent in my hand, lo! then, I drew out my own true blade and shook it flawless from hilt to point, gleaming white in that mist.

Therefore it sent a thrill of joy to my heart, to know that there was one friend left me yet. I sheathed it again carefully, and undoing it from my waist, hung it about my neck.

Then catching up my rags in my arms, I drew them up till my legs and feet were altogether clear from them, afterwards folded my arms over my breast, gave a long leap and ran, looking downward, but not giving heed to my way.

Once or twice I fell over stumps of trees, and such-like, for it was a cut-down wood that I was in, but I rose always, though bleeding and confused, and went on still, sometimes tearing madly through briars and gorse bushes, so that my blood dropped on the dead leaves as I went.

I ran in this way for about an hour; then I heard a gurgling and splashing of waters. I gave a great shout and leapt strongly, with shut eyes, and the black water closed over me.

When I rose again, I saw near me a boat with a man in it, but the shore was far off. I struck out towards the boat, but my clothes, which I had knotted and folded about me, weighed me down terribly.

The man looked at me, and began to paddle towards me with the oar he held in his left hand, having in his right a long, slender spear, barbed like a fish-hook. Perhaps, I thought, it is some fishing spear. Moreover his raiment was of scarlet, with upright stripes of yellow and black all over it.

When my eye caught his, a smile widened his mouth as if some one had made a joke; but I was beginning to sink, and indeed my head was almost under water just as he came and stood above me, but before it went quite under, I saw his spear gleam, then *felt* it in my shoulder, and for the present, felt nothing else.

When I woke I was on the bank of that river. The flooded waters went hurrying past me; no boat on them now. From the river the ground went up in gentle slopes till it grew a great hill, and there, on that hill-top— Yes, I might forget many things, almost everything, but not that, not the old castle of my fathers up among the hills, its towers blackened now and shattered, yet still no enemy's banner waved from it.

So I said I would go and die there; and at this thought I drew my sword, which yet hung about my neck, and shook it in the air till the true steel quivered, then began to pace towards the castle. I was quite naked, no rag about me. I took no heed of that, only thanking God that my sword was left, and so toiled up the hill. I entered the castle soon by the outer court. I knew the way so well that I did not lift my eyes from the ground, but walked on over the lowered drawbridge through the un-guarded gates, and stood in the great hall at last – my father's hall – as bare of everything but my sword as when I came into the world fifty years before: I had as little clothes, as little wealth, less memory and thought, I verily believe, than then.

So I lifted up my eyes and gazed; no glass in the windows, no hangings on the walls; the vaulting yet held good throughout, but seemed to be going; the mortar had fallen out from between the stones, and grass and ferns grew in the joints; the marble pavement was in some places gone, and water stood about in puddles, though one scarce knew how it had got there.

No hangings on the walls – yet, strange to say, instead of them, the walls blazed from end to end with scarlet paintings, only striped across with green damp-marks in many places, some falling bodily from the wall, the plaster hanging down with the fading colour on it.

In all of them, except for the shadows and the faces of the figures, there was scarce any colour but scarlet and yellow. Here and there it seemed the painter, whoever it was, had tried to make his trees or his grass green, but it would not do; some ghastly thoughts must have filled his head, for all the green went presently into yellow, out-sweeping through the picture dismally. But the faces were painted to the very life, or it seemed so – there were only five of them, however, that were very marked or came much in the foreground; and four of these I knew well, though I did not then remember the names of those that had borne them. They were Red Harald, Swanhilda, Arnald, and myself. The fifth I did not know; it was a woman's and very beautiful.

Then I saw that in some parts a small penthouse roof had been built over the paintings, to keep them from the weather. Near one of these stood a man painting, clothed in red, with stripes of yellow and black. Then I knew that it was the same man who had saved me from drowning by spearing me through the shoulder; so I went up to him, and saw furthermore that he was girt with a heavy sword.

He turned round when he saw me coming, and asked me fiercely what I did there.

I asked why he was painting in my castle.

Thereupon, with that same grim smile widening his mouth as heretofore, he said, 'I paint God's judgments.'

And as he spoke, he rattled the sword in his scabbard; but I said, 'Well, then, you paint them very badly. Listen, I know God's judgments much better than you do. See now; I will teach you God's judgments, and you shall teach me painting.'

While I spoke he still rattled his sword, and when I had done, shut his right eye tight, screwing his nose on one side; then said:

'You have got no clothes on, and may go to the Devil! What do *you* know about God's judgments?'

'Well, they are not all yellow and red, at all events; you ought to know better.'

He screamed out, 'O you fool! Yellow and red! Gold and blood, what do they make?'

'Well,' I said, 'what?'

'HELL!' And, coming close up to me, he struck me with his

open hand in the face, so that the colour with which his hand was smeared was dabbed about my face. The blow almost threw me down; and, while I staggered, he rushed at me furiously with his sword. Perhaps it was good for me that I had got no clothes on, for, being utterly unencumbered, I leapt this way and that, and avoided his fierce, eager strokes till I could collect myself somewhat; while he had a heavy scarlet cloak on that trailed on the ground, and which he often trod on, so that he stumbled.

He very nearly slew me during the first few minutes, for it was not strange that, together with other matters, I should have forgotten the art of fencing: but yet, as I went on, and sometimes bounded about the hall under the whizzing of his sword, as he rested sometimes, leaning on it, as the point sometimes touched my head and made my eyes start out, I remembered the old joy that I used to have, and the *swy, swy* of the sharp edge, as one gazed between one's horse's ears. Moreover, at last, one fierce swift stroke, just touching me below the throat, tore up the skin all down my body, and fell heavy on my thigh, so that I drew my breath in and turned white. Then first, as I swung my sword round my head, our blades met – oh! to hear that *tchink* again! – and I felt the notch my sword made in his, and swung out at him, but he guarded it and returned on me. I guarded right and left, and grew warm, and opened my mouth to shout, but knew not what to say; and our sword points fell on the floor together. Then, when we had panted awhile, I wiped from my face the blood that had been dashed over it, shook my sword and cut at him, then we spun round and round in a mad waltz to the measured music of our meeting swords, and sometimes either wounded the other somewhat but not much, till I beat down his sword on to his head, that he fell grovelling, but not cut through. Verily, thereupon my lips opened mightily with 'Mary rings!'

Then, when he had got to his feet, I went at him again, he staggering back, guarding wildly. I cut at his head; he put his sword up confusedly, so I fitted both hands to my hilt, and smote him mightily under the arm. Then his shriek mingled with my shout made a strange sound together; he rolled over and over, dead, as I thought.

I walked about the hall in great exultation at first, striking my sword point on the floor every now and then, till I grew faint with loss of blood; then I went to my enemy and stripped off some of his clothes to bind up my wounds withal; afterwards I found in a corner bread and wine, and I ate and drank thereof.

Then I went back to him, and looked, and a thought struck me, and I took some of his paints and brushes, and kneeling down, painted his face thus, with stripes of yellow and red, crossing each other at right angles; and in each of the squares so made I put a spot of black, after the manner of the painted letters in the prayer-books and romances when they are ornamented.

So I stood back as painters do, folded my arms, and admired my own handiwork. Yet there struck me as being something so utterly doleful in the man's white face, and the blood running all about him, and washing off the stains of paint from his face and hands, and splashed clothes, that my heart misgave me, and I hoped that he was not dead; I took some water from a vessel he had been using for his painting, and, kneeling, washed his face.

Was it some resemblance to my father's dead face, which I had seen when I was young, that made me pity him? I laid my hand upon his heart, and felt it beating feebly; so I lifted him up gently, and carried him towards a heap of straw that he seemed used to lie upon. There I stripped him and looked to his wounds, and used leech-craft, the memory of which God gave me for this purpose, I suppose, and within seven days I found that he would not die.

Afterwards, as I wandered about the castle, I came to a room in one of the upper stories, that had still the roof on, and windows in it with painted glass, and there I found green raiment and swords and armour, and I clothed myself.

So when he got well I asked him what his name was, and he me, and we both of us said, 'Truly I know not.' Then said I, 'But we must call each other some name, even as men call days.'

'Call me Swerker,' he said. 'Some priest I knew once had that name.'

'And me Wulf,' said I, 'though wherefore I know not.'

Then I tried to learn painting till I thought I should die, but at last learned it through very much pain and grief.

And, as the years went on and we grew old and grey, we painted purple pictures and green ones instead of the scarlet and yellow, so that the walls looked altered, and always we painted God's judgments.

And we would sit in the sunset and watch them with the golden light changing them, as we yet hoped God would change both us and our works.

Often too we would sit outside the walls and look at the trees and sky, and the ways of the few men and women we saw. Therefrom sometimes befell adventures.

Once there went past a great funeral of some king going to his own country, not as he had hoped to go, but stiff and colourless, spices filling up the place of his heart.

And first went by very many knights, with long bright hauberks on, that fell down before their knees as they rode, and they all had tilting-helms on with the same crest, so that their faces were quite hidden: and this crest was two hands clasped together tightly as though they were the hands of one praying forgiveness from the one he loves best; and the crest was wrought in gold.

Moreover, they had on over their hauberks surcoats which were half scarlet and half purple, strewn about with golden stars.

Also long lances, that had forked knights'-pennons, half purple and half scarlet, strewn with golden stars.

And these went by with no sound but the fall of their horse-hoofs.

And they went slowly, so slowly that we counted them all, five thousand five hundred and fifty-five.

Then went by many fair maidens whose hair was loose and yellow, and who were all clad in green raiment ungirded, and shod with golden shoes.

These also we counted, being 500; moreover some of the outermost of them, viz., one maiden to every twenty, had long silver trumpets, which they swung out to right and left, blowing them, and their sound was very sad.

Then many priests, and bishops, and abbots, who wore white albs and golden copes over them; and they all sang

- - -

together mournfully, '*Propter amnen Babylonis,*' and these were 300.

After that came a great knot of the lords, who wore tilting helmets and surcoats emblazoned with each one his own device; only each had in his hand a small staff two feet long whereon was a pennon of scarlet and purple. These also were 300.

And in the midst of these was a great car hung down to the ground with purple, drawn by grey horses whose trappings were half scarlet, half purple.

And on this car lay the king, whose head and hands were bare; and he had on him a surcoat, half purple and half scarlet, strewn with golden stars.

And his head rested on a tilting helmet, whose crest was the hands of one praying passionately for forgiveness.

But his own hands lay by his side as if he had just fallen asleep.

And all about the car were little banners, half purple and half scarlet, strewn with golden stars.

Then the King, who counted but as one, went by also.

And after him came again many maidens clad in ungirt white raiment strewn with scarlet flowers, and their hair was loose and yellow and their feet bare, and except for the falling of their feet and the rustle of the wind through their raiment, they went past quite silently. These also were 500.

Then lastly came many young knights with long bright hauberks falling over their knees as they rode, and surcoats, half scarlet and half purple, strewn with golden stars; they bore long lances with forked pennons which were half purple, half scarlet, strewn with golden stars; their heads and their hands were bare, but they bore shields, each one of them, which were of bright steel wrought cunningly in the midst of which that bearing of the two hands of one who prays for forgiveness; which was done in gold. These were but 500.

Then they all went by winding up and up the hill roads, and, when the last of them had departed out of our sight, we put down our heads and wept, and I said, 'Sing us one of the songs of the Hollow Land.'

Then he whom I had called Swerker put his hand into his bosom, and slowly drew out a long, long tress of black hair, and laid it on his knee and smoothed it, weeping on it. So then I left him there and went and armed myself, and brought armour for him.

And then came back to him and threw the armour down so that it clanged, and said:

'O! Harald, let us go!'

He did not seem surprised that I called him by the right name, but rose and armed himself, and then he looked a good knight; so we set forth.

And in a turn of the long road we came suddenly upon a most fair woman, clothed in scarlet, who sat and sobbed, holding her face between her hands, and her hair was very black.

And when Harald saw her, he stood and gazed at her for long through the bars of his helmet, then suddenly turned, and said:

'Florian, I must stop here. Do you go on to the Hollow Land. Farewell.'

'Farewell.' And then I went on, never turning back, and him I never saw more.

And so I went on, quite lonely, but happy, till I had reached the Hollow Land.

Into which I let myself down most carefully, by the jutting rocks and bushes and strange trailing flowers, and there lay down and fell asleep.

Third Canto

And I was waked by some one singing; I felt very happy; I felt young again; I had fair delicate raiment on, my sword was gone, and my armour. I tried to think where I was, and could not for my happiness; I tried to listen to the words of the song. Nothing, only an old echo in my ears, only all manner of strange scenes from my wretched past life before my eyes in a dim, far-off manner. Then at last, slowly, without effort, I heard what she sang.

> 'Christ keep the Hollow Land
>   All the summer-tide;
> Still we cannot understand
>   Where the waters glide;

Only dimly seeing them
Coldly slipping through
Many green-lipp'd cavern mouths
Where the hills are blue.

'Then,' she said, 'come now and look for it, love, a hollow city in the Hollow Land.'

I kissed Margaret, and we went.

Through the golden streets under the purple shadows of the houses we went, and the slow fanning backward and forward of the many-coloured banners cooled us: we two alone. There was no one with us; no soul will ever be able to tell what we said, how we looked.

At last we came to a fair palace, cloistered off in the old time, before the city grew golden from the din and hubbub of traffic; those who dwelt there in the old ungolden times had had their own joys, their own sorrows, apart from the joys and sorrows of the multitude. So, in like manner, was it now cloistered off from the eager leaning and brotherhood of the golden dwellings; so now it had its own gaiety, its own solemnity, apart from theirs; unchanged, unchangeable, were its marble walls, whatever else changed about it.

We stopped before the gates and trembled, and clasped each other closer; for there among the marble leafage and tendrils that were round and under and over the archway that held the golden valves, were wrought two figures of a man and woman, winged and garlanded, whose raiment flashed with stars; and their faces were like faces we had seen or half seen in some dream long and long and long ago, so that we trembled with awe and delight. And I turned, and seeing Margaret, saw that her face was that face seen or half seen long and long and long ago; and in the shining of her eyes I saw that other face, seen in that way and no other long and long and long ago – my face.

And then we walked together towards the golden gates, and opened them, and no man gainsaid us.

And before us lay a great space of flowers.